What Is Valentine's Day?

Harriet Ziefert • Pictures by Claire Schumacher

HarperFestival

A Division of HarperCollins*Publishers*

"Today is Valentine's Day," said Little Mouse's teacher. "We have to get ready."

"What is Valentine's Day?"
asked Little Mouse.

The teacher said, "On Valentine's Day we make cards for friends and relatives to tell them we love and care about them."

Everyone went right to work.

Little Mouse filled her knapsack with Valentines.

She gave one to her teacher.

Little Mouse gave Valentines to her friends.

There was one Valentine for the neighbor's rabbit...

one Valentine for Little Mouse's mommy…

Is there a Valentine for Little Mouse?

Happy Valentine's Day!